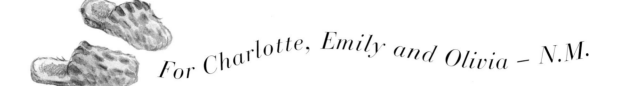

For Charlotte, Emily and Olivia – N.M.

To Louis – E.T.

Text copyright © 2004 by Nicola Moon
Illustrations copyright © 2004 by Eleanor Taylor

Published by Bloomsbury, New York and London
Distributed to the trade by Holtzbrinck Publishers
Library of Congress Cataloging-in-Publication Data
available upon request
ISBN 1-58234-944-4

First U.S. Edition

1 3 5 7 9 10 8 6 4 2

Bloomsbury USA Children's Books
175 Fifth Avenue
New York, NY 10010

TICK-TOCK, DRIP-DROP!

A BEDTIME STORY

BY
NICOLA MOON

ILLUSTRATED BY
ELEANOR TAYLOR

BLOOMSBURY
CHILDREN'S
BOOKS

Rabbit was lying in his bed, trying to get to sleep.

Tick-tock, tick-tock, went the clock.

"I can't get to sleep," said Rabbit. "All I can hear is that *tick-tock, tick-tock*. It's driving me mad."

"I'll stop the clock," said Mole,
and he got out of bed.

Rabbit plumped his pillows
and turned over.
"At last! No more *tick-tock*.
Now I can go to sleep."

Rabbit couldn't hear a *tick-tock*,
but he could hear a *drip-drop*.
Drip-drop, drip-drop, went the tap.

"I can't get to sleep," said Rabbit. "All I can hear is
that *drip-drop, drip-drop*. It's driving me mad."

"I'll turn off the tap," said Mole, and he got out of bed.

Rabbit turned over and sighed. "At last! No more *tick-tock*, *drip-drop*, now I can get to sleep!"

Rabbit couldn't hear
a *tick-tock, drip-drop,*
but he could
hear a *prr-prrr.*
Prr-prrr, prr-prrr,
went the cat.

"I can't get to sleep," said Rabbit. "All I can hear is that *prr-prrr, prr-prrr*. It's driving me mad."

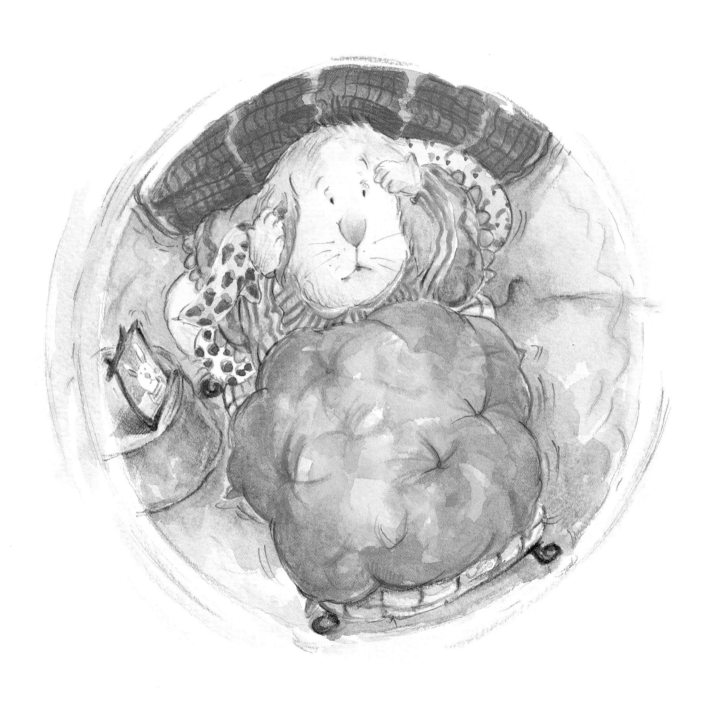

"I'll put the cat downstairs," said Mole, and he got out of bed.

Rabbit yawned and closed his eyes.
"At last! No more *tick-tock*, *drip-drop*,
prr-prrr, now I can get to sleep."

Rabbit couldn't hear a *tick-tock*,
drip-drop, *prr-prrr*, but he
could hear a *bang-bump*.
Bang-bump, *bang-bump*,
went the garden gate
in the wind.

"I can't get to sleep," said Rabbit.
"All I can hear is that *bang-bump*,
bang-bump. It's driving me mad."
"You're driving me mad, but
I'll close the gate," said Mole,
and he got out of bed.

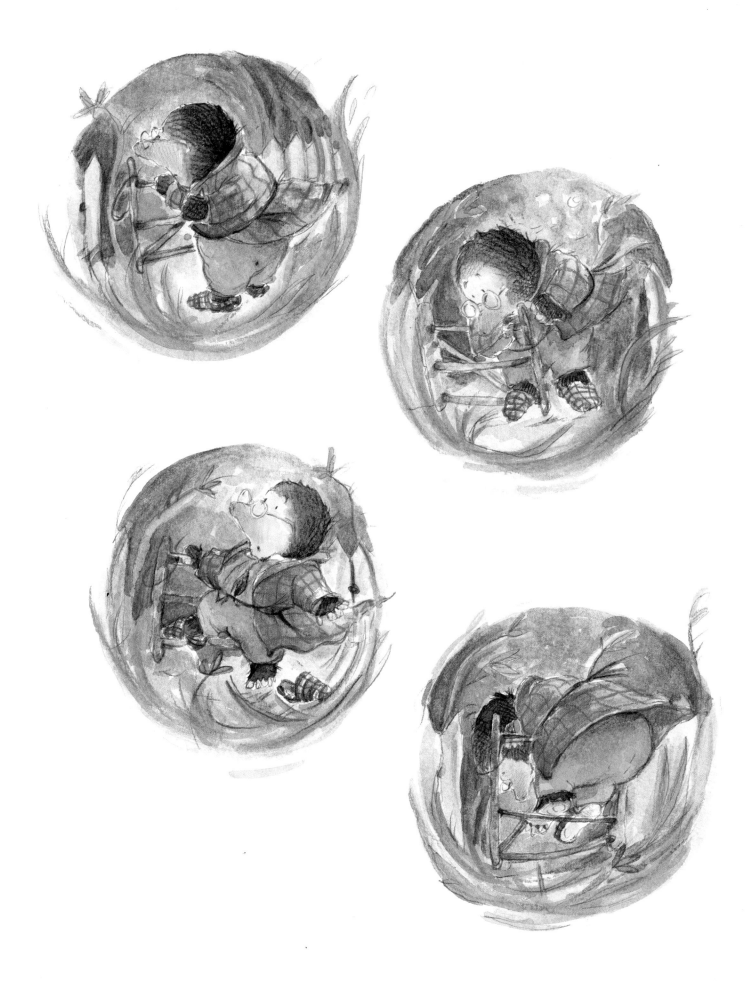

Rabbit pulled the bedclothes up round his neck
and stretched out his legs.

"That's better! *Now* I can get to sleep!" he said.

Rabbit couldn't hear
a *tick-tock, drip-drop,*
prr-prrr, bang-bump.
He couldn't hear
anything at all.
Just silence.

And he fell sound asleep.
"At last!" said Mole.

Mole lay in his bed
trying to get to sleep.
Snore-snore,
snore-snore,
went Rabbit.

"Now *I* can't get to sleep,"
said Mole. "All I can hear is
that *snore-snore, snore-snore.*
It's driving me mad."

So he got out of his bed, took his blanket and pillow,
and went downstairs to sleep with the cat.

No *tick-tock*, no *drip-drop*,
no *bang-bump*,
no *snore-snore*.
Just a gentle
prr-prrr,
prr-prrr,
prr-prrr . . .

And Mole fell fast asleep.